The Pied Piper

Retold by Alan Benjamin
Illustrated by Richard Walz

Based on a poem by Robert Browning

A GOLDEN BOOK • NEW YORK
Western Publishing Company, Inc., Racine, Wisconsin 53404

© 1991 Western Publishing Company, Inc. Illustrations © 1991 Richard Walz. All rights reserved. Printed in the U.S.A. No part of this book may be reproduced or copied in any form without written permission from the publisher. All trademarks are the property of Western Publishing Company, Inc. Library of Congress Catalog Card Number: 90-86139 ISBN: 0-307-00300-0   MCMXCII

The town of Hamelin lay along the bank of
a wide river. Its twisting streets were lined with
the comfortable houses of the happy people
who lived there. Life had gone on peacefully
and pleasantly in Hamelin for as long as
anyone could remember.

And then one day *rats* began to appear. At first there were only a few, and no one minded very much. In fact, the town's cats couldn't have been happier. But the rats multiplied, and soon there were more rats than townsfolk.

The rats were everywhere. After a while, folks didn't even feel safe in their own homes. The rats ate everything they could find.

Sometimes people were awakened in the middle of the night by rats about to nibble on their toes!

Finally the people of Hamelin were at their wits'
end. Off they marched to the town hall to see the
mayor. The mayor was a greedy man. He cared a
great deal about money but very little about
Hamelin's citizens.

"The rats are eating us out of house and home!"
cried an angry woman in the crowd.

The mayor told the townspeople to be patient, that he was doing all he could to help.

"Get rid of the rats—and soon—or we'll get rid of you!" shouted the town's banker.

The mayor was upset. Later, when he met with his council members, one of them said, "We've tried poison and traps, but we haven't caught any rats."

"Well, think of something that *will* work," the mayor thundered, "or we'll all be out of our jobs!"

Suddenly there was a tapping at the door. In stepped the oddest-looking fellow any of the council members had ever seen. He was as tall and as lean as a birch tree, with long sharp features and bright eyes as blue as sapphires. His clothes were a marvelous patchwork of color, and in his hand he carried a musical pipe.

"Who are you?" barked the mayor.

"I'm only a poor piper," answered the stranger, "but I can pipe music that will charm any living creature. If you will pay me a thousand guilders, I will get rid of the rats."

"If you can really do as you say, I'll give you fifty thousand guilders!" cried the mayor.

"Then play I shall," said the piper as he stepped
outside. He raised his pipe to his lips, and out came
a melody both strange and beautiful. No one had
ever heard music quite like it.

As the piper piped, out came the rats—big ones and small ones, fat ones and thin ones—till Hamelin's streets were filled with them. The rats followed the piper as he made his way through town, while the people watched in wonder.

When the piper came to the bank of the river, he stopped, but he continued to play his pipe. The rats, however, did not stop. Into the river they plunged— never to return to the town.

Hamelin was free of vermin at last. The people cheered as the piper made his way back to the town hall.

"I've come to collect my thousand guilders," he told the mayor.

"But I was only joking," said the mayor, chuckling. Now that the rats were gone, he had no further need for the piper. "I'll give you these fifty guilders and nothing more. Now take them and leave."

"Then leave I shall," said the piper, "but not before I've played a different tune." And he stepped outside and lifted his pipe once more.

As the music began the pattering of feet could be heard. But this time it was not the rats. From every corner of Hamelin came the children of the town. Hand in hand, dancing and prancing, the children followed the piper as he led them through the town.

When parents recognized their children in the procession, they tried to stop them but could not. The music had frozen the parents in place like statues.

On went the piper and his army of children, through the streets and over the bridge that led out of town. The last in line was a little lame boy. The tapping of his cane as he hurried to keep up with the others was the last sound the stricken townsfolk heard as their children disappeared from view.

When they could move again, the townsfolk rushed across the bridge to find the children. Following the road that led from Hamelin, they soon came to a mountain that the children had climbed.

There they found the little lame boy in tears. He told them that when the piper and the children had reached this place, a door in the mountain had opened up, and everyone had entered. Everyone, that is, except the boy himself. "I could not keep up with the others," he told the grown-ups sadly. "The door closed before I could reach it."

"Did the piper say where he was taking our children?" someone asked.

"Yes," the boy replied. "To a happy land where it is always spring. To a land of flowers and fountains, peacocks and winged horses."

The people stood and wept. Some pleaded with the mountain to open. Others shouted for the piper to return, promising that the mayor would pay what was owed him—and more.

But the mountain did not open, and the piper did not answer.

Let us all, dear reader, think well before we make promises we do not plan to keep. If, in our greed, we give less than we promised, we may get more than we bargained for.